The Besties to the Rescue

COLLECT ALL THE BOOKS IN THE SERIES!

Felice Arena + Tom Jellett

Will the besties be the BEST bird-parents EVER?

Felice Arena + Tom Jellett

Can the besties turn a very bad school day into the VERY BEST?

THE BESTIES make a splash

Felice Arena + Tom Jellett

COMING SOON
What if your bestie is having MORE FUN at the beach with someone else?

THE BESTIES party on

Felice Arena + Tom Jellett

COMING SOON
How will the besties' real party EVER compete with their AWESOME practice party?

MEET THE BESTIES!

PUFFIN BOOKS

UK | USA | Canada | Ireland | Australia
India | New Zealand | South Africa | China

Penguin Random House Australia is part of the Penguin Random House
group of companies whose addresses can be found at
global.penguinrandomhouse.com.

First published by Puffin Books, an imprint of
Penguin Random House Australia Pty Ltd, in 2020

Printed and bound in Australia by Griffin Press, an accredited
ISO AS/NZS 14001 Environmental Management Systems printer

 A catalogue record for this
book is available from the
National Library of Australia

ISBN 978 1 76 089097 1 (Paperback)

Penguin Random House Australia uses papers that are natural and recyclable
products, made from wood grown in sustainable forests. The logging and
manufacture processes are expected to conform to the environmental
regulations of the country of origin.

penguin.com.au

THE BESTIES
to the rescue

Felice Arena

ILLUSTRATED BY
Tom Jellett

PUFFIN BOOKS

CHAPTER ONE

BOING!

Ruby bounced on the trampoline.

BOING!

She jumped so high she
could see right over the
fence into Oliver's yard.
'Oliver!' she called.

BOING!
BOING!

'Hey, Ollie!'

BOING!

Oliver and Ruby had
been besties forever!

Ruby could see Oliver
in his treehouse. He was
listening to music and
drawing one of his amazing
comics.

He looked up and waved.

'Hi, Ollie!' Ruby yelled.
'I need your help! Could you
bring over your mum's old
phone?'

'Wait a minute, Rubes,' Oliver called. 'I'll just finish drawing these dinosaurs.'

Ruby guessed that she could do a straddle jump, a back drop and a forward spring by the time Oliver got there.

⑨

She was right!

'Could you record me?'
Ruby said. 'I'm going to do
something totally awesome!'

CHAPTER TWO

'Those jumps were amazing,' said Oliver. 'You were almost flying.'

'That's nothing!' Ruby said. 'I'm going to do a double back flip and a double forward flip.

All in one go.'

'That *is* awesome,' said
Oliver. 'I'll record it in slow
motion. It will look more
dramatic.'

Ruby took a deep breath.
'Ready, set . . . GO!'

BOING! **FLIP!**

Ruby tucked her knees
to her chest and flipped
backwards. Her hair
was flying **BOING!**
everywhere.

She followed that up with
a giant straddle leap . . .

. . . and finished with two
forward flips.

'Did you get all that,
Ollie?' she asked excitedly.

The besties replayed the video.

'Slow-mo is sooo good,' said Ruby.

But Oliver wasn't watching Ruby's jumping.

'Look!' he said. 'In the background. Behind you!'

Oliver paused the video
and zoomed into the corner
of the screen.

A big fat ginger cat was
sitting on the back fence
watching a bird's nest.

'It's Cutie Pie,' said Ruby.

'She lives across the road.'

The besties watched
Cutie Pie pounce on the
nest in slow motion.

The grown-up bird
flew away, and a little
bird fell to the ground.

㉑

CHAPTER THREE

'Oh no!' the besties gasped.

They ran quickly to help.

Cutie Pie jumped down beside them. She leaned against Ruby's leg, purring loudly.

Ruby pushed her away.

'How could you,
Cutie Pie?' she said.

'It's not her fault,' Oliver
said. 'Cats eat birds.
They're predators. It's what
they do.'

He knelt down to look in
the bushes. 'Here he is.'

Oliver gently scooped the
baby sparrow into his cap.

But Cutie Pie was still
there, and she still seemed
very interested . . .

'Look out!' Ruby cried.

Oliver leapt into action.

He turned and . . .

CHAPTER FOUR

Cutie Pie hissed and raced
off.

Ruby cheered. 'You really did sound barking mad,' she said. 'Get it?'

Oliver laughed. 'Yep! But that was a close call!'

Ruby looked at the little bird and sighed. 'Thank goodness he's not hurt. He's a baby sparrow, a fledgling – he was almost ready to leave the nest.'

Oliver looked surprised.

'How do you know that,
Rubes?'

'You're not the only one
who knows about animals,'
Ruby said, sticking out her
tongue.

'Well, since Cutie Pie wants to eat him, there's only one thing we can do,' said Oliver.

Ruby nodded. '*We* have to eat him first.'

'What?' Oliver cried. 'NO!'

'I'm only joking, Ollie!'
Ruby laughed. 'As if! Let's
look after him until he's
ready to fly.'

CHAPTER FIVE

The little sparrow chirped. He flapped his wings, but he still couldn't fly away.

'We'll have to keep an eye on him all the time,' said Ruby.

Oliver gently put the
little bird back on the grass.

'If his parents don't come
back soon, he won't have
any food.'

'Ta da!' Ruby pulled a packet of chips out of her jacket pocket.

'Oh, Rubes! He can't eat that,' said Oliver.

'I know,' Ruby said, stuffing a handful of chips in her mouth.

'But I can! All this talk about food is making me hungry.'

CRUNCH!
CRUNCH!
CRUNCH!

'Can you crunch a little softer?' said Oliver. 'I think you're scaring him . . .'

Oliver's tummy made a hungry noise.

'They do look good. Can I have some?'

Ruby nodded.

'I know,' she said. 'I'll play our baby bird a song.'

She picked up her uke and started to strum.

'Little bird, little bird, it's lucky you're not dead . . . and Cutie Pie didn't bite off your head.'

'It's a great song, Rubes, but now he looks even more scared,' said Oliver.

'Hey, Rubes. Do you think he'd like us to give him a name?' asked Oliver.

'That's a great idea,' Ruby said.

The besties sat and looked at the little sparrow.

Finally Oliver smiled.

'I know!' he said. 'What
about Rex?'

'That's cool!' said Ruby.
'But why Rex?'

'As in T-rex,' said Oliver.
'Because birds are related
to dinosaurs.'

'Imagine if we really were looking after a baby dinosaur – a little T-rex,' said Ruby.

Oliver pulled out his notepad and started to draw . . .

Suddenly Rex started
flipping and flopping,
flapping and fluttering.

'He loves his name!'
cried Ruby.

'I think he does,' said Oliver. 'But I think he might also be trying to fly.'

Ruby was so excited she started singing.

'Little bird, little bird, it's time, little guy. Little bird, little bird, it's time to fly.'

'Come on, Rex,' said Oliver. 'You can do it.'

CHAPTER SIX

But Rex just spread his wings and chirped.

'He doesn't know how,' said Oliver. 'His parents aren't here to teach him.'

The besties looked at each other.

'We can teach him!' they said at the same time.

'You can show him on the tramp, Rubes,' said Oliver.

Oliver held the baby
sparrow, while Ruby climbed
onto the trampoline.

'Right! I'm ready to go,'
she said, lightly bouncing
on her toes. 'I hope you are
too, Rex. Watch and learn!'

'Make sure you jump as high as you can, Rubes,' Oliver said. 'And then I'll release Rex.'

'Got it! Okay, here goes,'
Ruby said.

She started to jump.

Ruby bounced higher, and
higher, and higher.

'Woo-hoo!'

Oliver held Rex up, just
as Ruby reached the highest
she'd ever jumped . . .

Rex flapped his wings
and took off.

He flew up and up and
up, out over the rooftops,
until the besties could
no longer see him.

'Yeah!' they cheered.
'We did it. We did it!'

Oliver scrambled up onto
the trampoline and joined
Ruby.

And together they jumped for joy – and for Rex.

HOW TO LOOK AFTER
A BABY BIRD

Step 1.   If you find a baby bird on the ground, check for any cats or dogs and keep them away if you can.

Step 2.   Move away for a while. The parents might be ready to take care of their baby, but they might be too scared of you.

Step 3.   You can move a fledgling to a more protected spot (like the bushes) if you think it's in danger.

Step 4.   If the little bird is injured or it doesn't have many feathers (meaning it's very young), then it needs help. You can call a vet or a wildlife-care group for advice.

Step 5. If you need to move an injured bird, place it in a small box with something soft inside. Take it to a warm, dark, quiet place.

Step 6. Keep an eye on your fledgling until the parents find it or it flies away.

Step 7. If that doesn't happen by night time, then call a wildlife-care group for advice.

Step 8. Give yourself a pat on the back for being a wildlife protector!

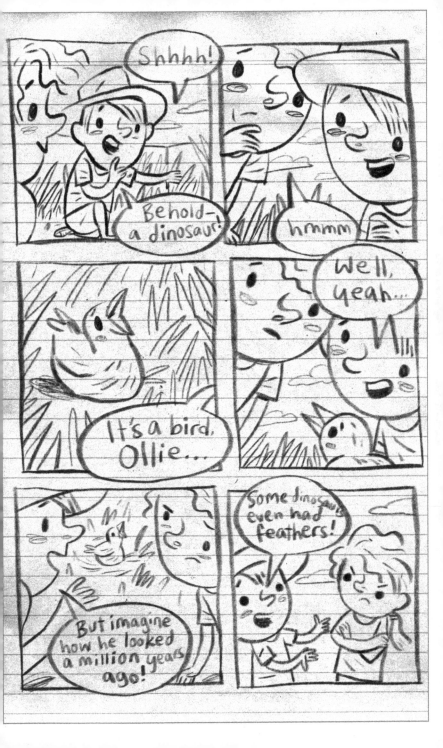

MY SONG – LITTLE BIRD

Here are the chords I used to play this song on the uke:

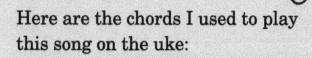

A7   D7   B   E7

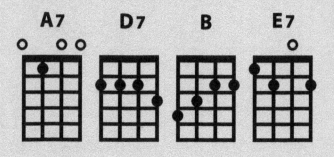

A7
I found myself a cute little sparrow.
  D7
It had fallen from its nest out of a tree.
        B   E7
But what troubles me, it's lost its parents.
A7   D7   A7
How desperate must this little bird be?

B
Little bird, little bird,

E7
it's lucky you're not dead,

A7   D7   A7
and Cutie Pie didn't bite off your head.

      A7
Little bird, little bird, it's time, little guy.

      D7
Little bird, little bird, it's time to fly.

      B   E7
Little bird, little bird, I'll try not to cry

      B   E7
Little bird, little bird, please try not to die.

      A7   D7   A7
Little bird, little bird, little bird.

To hear this song and for all the
lyrics, a full chord sheet and
the strumming patterns go to
TheBestiesWorld.com

See you there!

Ruby

THE BESTIES' BEST JOKES!

What do you call a dinosaur
with no eyes?
Doyouthinkysaraus?

What do you call a sleeping
dinosaur?
A dino-snore!

What is a hungry T-rex's
favourite number?
Eight (ate!)

What did the dinosaur put
on her steak?
Dinosauce!

What do you call a dinosaur that
destroys everything?
Tyrannosaurus wrecks!

MEET THE SPORTY KIDS!

If you loved meeting the besties you'll love hanging out with the sporty kids . . .